SCREEEEEEEEEEEEEEEEEEE!

SCREECHY KEEN

TERRANCE GRIEP, JR. - WRITER * KAREN MATCHETTE - PENCILLER * DAVE HUNT - INKER
TOM ORZECHOWSKI - LETTERER * PAUL BECTON - COLORIST * DIGITAL CHAMELEON - SEPARATIONS
HARVEY RICHARDS - ASSISTANT EDITOR * JOAN HILTY - EDITOR

Spotlight

## VISIT US AT
## www.abdopublishing.com

Reinforced library bound edition published in 2010 by Spotlight, a division of the ABDO Group, 8000 West 78th Street, Edina, Minnesota 55439. Spotlight produces high-quality reinforced library bound editions for schools and libraries. Published by agreement with Warner Bros.—A Time Warner Company. All rights reserved. Used under authorization.

Printed in the United States of America, Melrose Park, Illinois.
092009
012010

 PRINTED ON RECYCLED PAPER

**Library of Congress Cataloging-in-Publication Data**

Griep, Terrance.
   Scooby-Doo in Screechy keen / writer, Terrance Griep, Jr. ; penciller, Karen Matchette ; inker, Dave Hunt ; colorist, Paul Becton ; letterer, Tom Orzechowski. -- Reinforced library bound ed.
      p. cm. -- (Scooby-Doo graphic novels)
   ISBN 978-1-59961-697-1
   1. Graphic novels.  I. Matchette, Karen. II. Scooby-Doo (Television program) III. Title. IV. Title: Screechy keen!
   PZ7.7.G75Sc 2010
   741.5'973--dc22

                              2009032902

All Spotlight books have reinforced library bindings and
are manufactured in the United States of America.

# SCREECHY KEEN

OKAY, SCOOBY, LET'S SOUND-CHECK THIS GROOVY, HI-FI *SURVEILLANCE EQUIPMENT!* SO MAKE LIKE A FIELD MOUSE, AND WE'LL FIND OUT IF I CAN, LIKE, PICK UP THE SQUEAK...

RI ROT RHE RUNCHIES!

TERRANCE GRIEP, JR. - WRITER * KAREN MATCHETTE - PENCILLER * DAVE HUNT - INKER
TOM ORZECHOWSKI - LETTERER * PAUL BECTON - COLORIST * DIGITAL CHAMELEON - SEPARATIONS
HARVEY RICHARDS - ASSISTANT EDITOR * JOAN HILTY - EDITOR

YEAH, LIKE, I'VE GOT THE MUNCHIES, *TOO!*

AHEE HEEHEEHEE!

SHAGGY-- WE GOT THAT *EXPANDER* TO RECORD AND PLAY BACK SOUNDS FOR INVESTIGATIONS, NOT FOR *FUN!*

AWW, VELMA...

OVER A THOUSAND YEARS AGO, THE EMPEROR OF CHINA POSSESSED A MYSTERIOUS GLOWING GREEN STONE, FILLED WITH GREAT POWER, CALLED **THE DRAGON'S EYE.**

THE EMPEROR CUT THE STONE INTO SEVEN SMALLER, INTERLOCKING STONES, WHICH HE DISTRIBUTED AMONG HIS SONS. OVER TIME, THE STONES WERE SCATTERED AROUND THE WORLD.

NOW, SOME MYSTERIOUS VILLAIN IS STEALING THESE STONES. HE'S OUTWITTED THE GANG IN PARIS, MOSCOW, ROME, DAMASCUS, THE FORESTS OF INDIA, AND THE SEA OF JAPAN, BUT WILL HE BEAT THEM IN...

THE IMPERIAL PALACE, "THE FORBIDDEN CITY" PEKING, CHINA.

YOU YOUNGSTERS HAVE **NOTHING** TO WORRY ABOUT.

THE THEFT OF SIX OTHER SECTIONS OF THE DRAGON'S EYE WAS **INTERNATIONAL NEWS.**

AS SOON AS THE SECOND PIECE WAS STOLEN IN RUSSIA, WE MADE PREPARATIONS TO SAFEGUARD THE SECTION THAT IS HOUSED HERE.

AS YOU KNOW, THE DRAGON'S EYE HAS CULTURAL SIGNIFICANCE TO THE PEOPLE OF CHINA. WE HAVE EVERY INTENTION OF MAKING CERTAIN THAT IT **REMAINS** IN **CHINA.**

WELL, Mr. WU, WE BELIEVE THAT THAT'S THE THIEF'S MOTIVE AS WELL.

WE THINK THAT HE WANTS **ALL** OF THE PIECES OF THE DRAGON'S EYE TO BE KEPT IN CHINA-- BUT I DOUBT THAT **HERE** IN THE IMPERIAL PALACE IS WHERE HE'S PLANNING TO KEEP THEM!